BOX AND COX

by Grace Chetwin

illustrated by David Small

Bradbury Press
New York

Bradbury Press
An Affiliate of Macmillan, Inc.
866 Third Avenue, New York, NY 10022
Collier Macmillan Canada, Inc.

The text of this book is set in Bodoni.
The illustrations are rendered in pen-and-ink and gouache.
Typography by Julie Quan

Printed and bound in Hong Kong
First American Edition

10   9   8   7   6   5   4   3   2   1

Library of Congress Cataloging-in-Publication Data
Chetwin, Grace.
Box and Cox / by Grace Chetwin ; illustrated by David Small. — 1st ed.
p.   cm.
Summary: The adventures of Box, a printer, and Cox, a hatter, who are
always in the same place but never at the same time.
ISBN 0-02-718314-9
[1. Humorous stories.]   I. Small, David, 1945-   ill.   II. Title.
PZ7.C42555Bo   1990
[E]—dc19   88-35337   CIP   AC

For Barbara, with love
Special thanks to the first grade children of
the Gribbin School, Glen Cove, New York, and
to those young readers of the Bayville Free Library
who shared the fun in making this tale.
—G.C.

For Sherry
—D.S.

Box is a journeyman printer.

Cox is a journeyman hatter.

Box works at Caleb Fudge's
Banner Press on Main Street.

Cox works at Jebediah Tippet's
Hat Emporium on Main Street.

Box works nights.
And Cox works days.

Box rents a room,
second floor rear,
in Mrs. Bouncer's house
on Third Street.

Cox rents a room,
second floor rear,
in Mrs. Bouncer's house
on Third Street.

It is the same room.
But they don't know it.

It is Box's during the day.
And Cox's during the night.
Mrs. Bouncer has rented it to both.
Waste not, want not is her motto.
She's a widow, and she needs the money.

She earns it.

Every morning, after Cox goes out to work, Mrs. Bouncer takes out Cox's things, and puts in Box's before Box comes back home to sleep.

Every evening, after Box goes out to work, Mrs. Bouncer takes out Box's things, and puts in Cox's before Cox comes back home to sleep.

She keeps the things in the broom closet
on the landing next to her room. She hangs
dressing gown, suits, on a rail.

She piles socks, shirts, and ties on the shelf.
She puts toothbrush, hairbrush, and pictures
off the wall in a crate on the floor.

Every morning, she gives Cox breakfast before he goes out.

Every morning, she gives Box breakfast after he comes in.

Every evening, she gives Box supper before he goes out.

Every evening, she gives Cox supper after he comes in.

Box is happy with his room. "Oh, Mrs. Bouncer," sighs Box as he pays his rent. "I couldn't be happier."

Cox is happy with his room. "Oh, Mrs. Bouncer," sighs Cox as he pays his rent. "I couldn't be happier."

Mrs. Bouncer is happy with her two tenants.
"Oh, my," she says as she counts the rents.
"I couldn't be happier."

One morning, as he is going home from work, Box goes
to buy himself a new hat at Jebediah Tippet's Hat Emporium.

"Good morning, sir," says Cox. "What can I do for you?"

"Sell me a new hat, and quickly, please, so I can go home,"
says Box. "I work long nights, you see."

"Work nights!" yawns Cox. "How do you do it?"
He finds Box a hat and Box goes home happy.

One evening, as he is going home from work, Cox goes
to buy a magazine at Caleb Fudge's Banner Press.

"Good evening, sir," says Box. "What can I do for you?"

"Sell me a magazine, and quickly, please, so I can go home,"
says Cox. "I work long days, you see."

"Work days!" Box yawns. "How do you do it?"
He finds Cox a magazine and Cox goes home happy.

And so everyone is happy and life is quiet until one day, at breakfast, Cox says, "Dear Mrs. Bouncer. I've been thinking. Will you marry me?"

Mrs. Bouncer is flustered. She cannot say no. "Thank you," she says. "That would be nice."

Cox goes out to work, whistling.

When Box comes in to breakfast, he says,
"Dear Mrs. Bouncer, I've been thinking.
Will you marry me?"

Mrs. Bouncer is flustered. She cannot say no.
"Thank you," she says. "That would be nice."

Box goes to sleep, whistling.

Mrs. Bouncer stands and wrings her hands.
"Oh, what a pickle I am in," she says. "It is one thing
to rent the same room to Mr. Box and Mr. Cox at the same time.
But promise to marry them both? Whatever shall I do?"
She puts on her hat and goes to buy supper.
To celebrate his engagement, Cox's boss
gives him the day off.

Cox comes home.

Cox walks into his room. He stops and looks around in amazement. Everything is changed.

It is not his dressing gown behind the door.

That is not his hairbrush on the dresser.

Those are not his pictures on the wall.

And there is a stranger in his bed.

"Well, I never!" Cox cries out loud. Is he in the wrong room?

Box wakes up.

"Well, I never!" Box cries out loud. "Who are you?"

"I'm Cox!" cries Cox. "Who are you?"

"I'm Box," cries Box. "What are you doing here?
This is my room. Mrs. Bouncer rented it to me."

"Oh?" cries Cox. "This is my room. Mrs. Bouncer rented it to me!"

"Well, I never!" they both cry together. "She's rented
the room to us both!"

Now what will they do?

"I know," says Cox. "Mrs. Bouncer has promised to marry me. I won't need this room. You can keep it."

"Marry you?" cries Box. "Mrs. Bouncer has promised to marry me!"

"Well, I never!" they both cry together. "She's promised to marry us both!"

They dash to Mrs. Bouncer's room.

They open the broom closet door by mistake, and
find Cox's things inside: dressing gown and suits on the rail;
socks, shirts, and ties on the shelf; toothbrush, hairbrush,
and pictures off the wall in the crate on the floor.

"Well, I never!" cries Box.
He packs up his things, and leaves.

"Well, I never!" cries Cox.
He packs up his things, and leaves.

Mrs. Bouncer comes home
to an empty house.

At first, she is upset,
but after a cup of tea,
she begins to feel relieved.

No more running up and down stairs. No more worry
over which man to wed. Her troubles are over.
But she still needs the rent.

So Mrs. Bouncer hangs out her sign again: